For Hazel Beatrice, who likes to lick the bowl —E.J.

For Tom and Amie, who took me to pick blackberries at the golden end of summer —S.B.

Acknowledgments

Thanks for assistance with the author's research goes to: Francine Segan, author of *Shakespeare's Kitchen* and *The Philosopher's Kitchen*, among other food history books; Cathy Kaufman at Culinary Historians of New York; Amy Bentley at New York University; Ayun Halliday; and Lynn Olver at Foodtimeline.org.

 Published in the United States by
Schwartz & Wade Books,
an imprint of Random House Children's Books,
a division of Random House LLC, a Penguin Random House Company, New York.
Schwartz & Wade Books and the colophon are
trademarks of Random House LLC.
Visit us on the Web! randomhousekids.com
Educators and librarians, for a variety of teaching tools,
visit us at RHTeachersLibrarians.com

Library of Congress Cataloging-in-Publication Data
Jenkins, Emily.
A fine dessert / by Emily Jenkins ; illustrated by Sophie Blackall.—1st ed.
p. cm.
Summary: Depicts families, from England to California and from 1710 to 2010, preparing and enjoying the dessert called blackberry fool. Includes a recipe and historical notes.
ISBN 978-0-375-86832-0 (trade) — ISBN 978-0-375-96832-7 (glb)
ISBN 978-0-375-98771-7 (ebook)
[1. Desserts—Fiction. 2. Cooking—Fiction. 3. Blackberries—Fiction.]
I. Blackall, Sophie, ill. II. Title.
PZ7.J4134Fhn 2015 [E]—dc23 2011023589

The text of this book is set in Archetype.
The illustrations were rendered in Chinese ink, watercolor, and blackberry juice on paper.
MANUFACTURED IN CHINA
2 4 6 8 10 9 7 5 3 1

First Edition

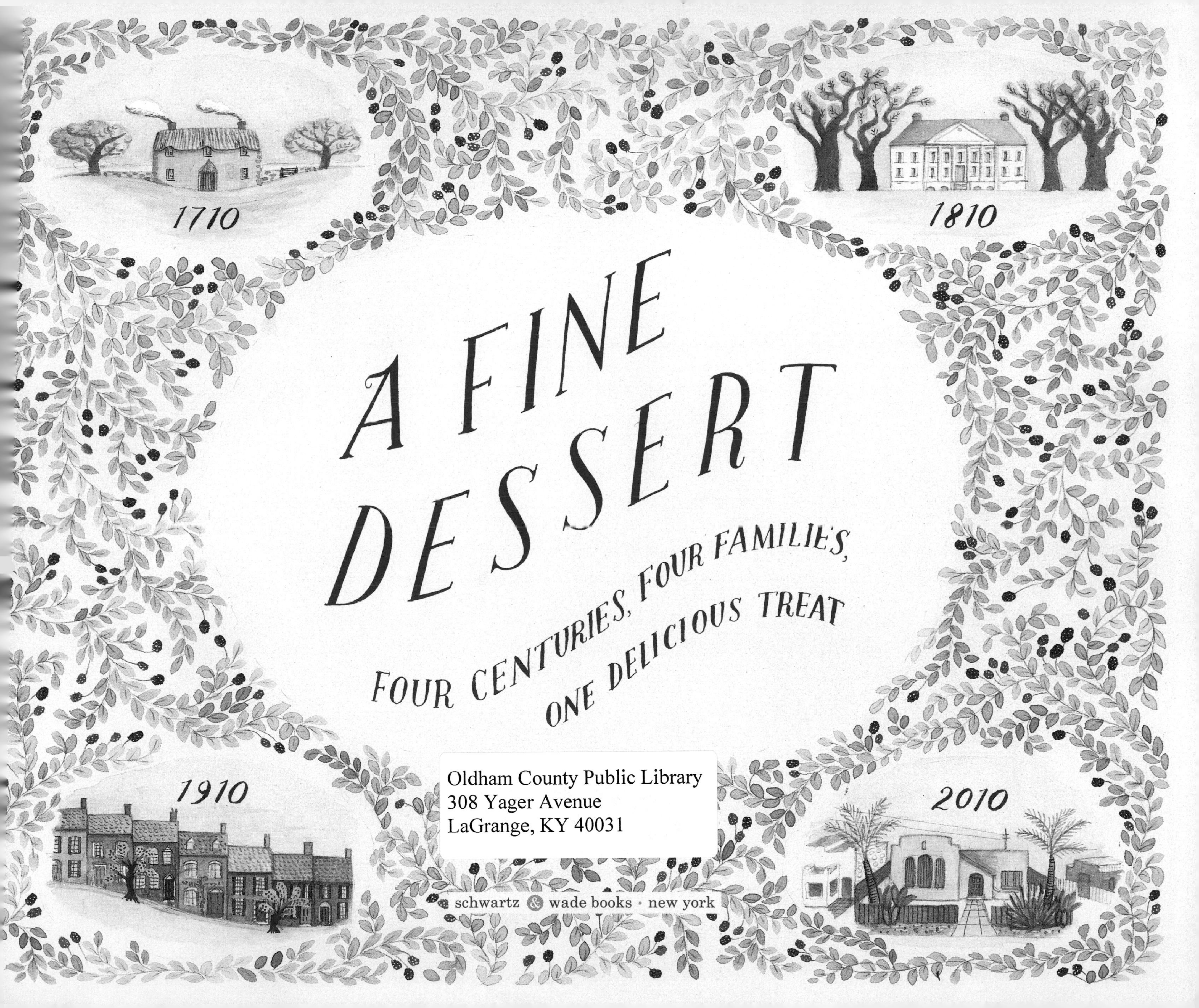
1710
1810
A FINE DESSERT
FOUR CENTURIES, FOUR FAMILIES,
ONE DELICIOUS TREAT
1910
2010
schwartz & wade books · new york

A bit more than three hundred years ago, in an English town called Lyme, a girl and her mother picked wild blackberries. Their hands turned purple with the juice. The thorns of the berry bushes pricked the fabric of their long skirts.

When they got home, the woman skimmed the cream off the evening's milk. She added it to the cream from the morning's milk and began to beat it all with a bundle of clean, soft twigs.

Beat beat.
Beat beat.
Beat beat.

Her arm
began
to ache.

Beat beat.
Beat beat.
Fifteen minutes later,
she stopped.
Whipped cream.

The girl drew water from the well.

She put the berries in a piece of muslin and rinsed them.

Then she squashed and strained them through the muslin, getting rid of the seeds.

Together, she and her mother poured sugar on the fruit and then mixed it with the cream.

"You may lick the spoon, love," said the woman.

So the girl did.

Mmmmm.

They carried the mixture to an ice pit in the hillside.
It chilled near sheets of winter ice, packed with reeds and straw.

ABCDEFGHIJ
KLMNOPQRS
TUVWXYZ
0123456789&
What is dark with-
in me, illumine.

After the family supper—cold chicken,
mushroom ketchup and meat pie—
they spooned the blackberry fool into blue dishes
and served it to Father and the older brothers.
Even the baby had some.

Mmmmm. Mmmmm. Mmmmm.

Later in the kitchen, the girl licked the bowl clean.

What a fine dessert!

A bit more than two hundred years ago, outside a city called Charleston, South Carolina, a girl and her mother picked blackberries from the plantation garden.

A horse-drawn wagon delivered cream from a nearby dairy.

The girl beat the cream with a metal whisk made by the local blacksmith.

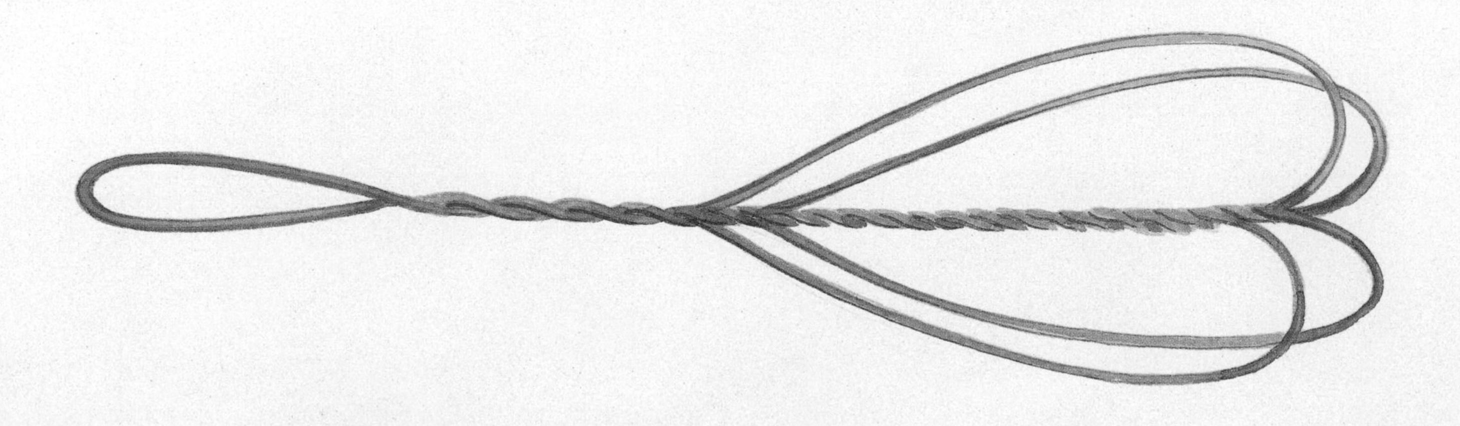

Beat beat.
Beat beat.

Her arm
began
to ache.
Beat beat.

Ten minutes later:
whipped cream.

The girl washed the berries in water from the well. Then she smashed them through a tin sieve with the back of a spoon, getting rid of the seeds.

Together, she and her mother poured sugar on the fruit and then mixed it with the cream.

"You may lick the spoon, child," the woman said.

So the girl did.

Mmmmm.

They carried the mixture to a wooden box in the basement. It was stacked with blocks of ice, lined with lead and insulated with cork. They put the bowl in.

After waiting table at supper—where
the master and his family ate turtle
soup, roast turkey, corn cakes and sweet
potatoes—they spooned the blackberry
fool into yellow dishes and served it.

Later, the girl and her mother
hid in the closet and licked
the bowl clean together.
Mmmmm. Mmmmm. Mmmmm.
What a fine dessert!

A bit more than one hundred years ago, in a city called Boston, Massachusetts, a girl and her mother bought two wooden boxes of blackberries at an open-air market.

When they got home, their morning's delivery of pasteurized cream was waiting at the door in pretty glass bottles.

The woman looked
at a recipe book.

She beat the cream with
cast-iron rotary beaters.
Whirrr. Whirrr.

Five minutes later:
whipped cream.

The girl drew water from the new
faucet in the kitchen. She washed
the berries and smashed them
through a sieve with her fingers. Her
hands turned purple with the juice.
Together, she and her mother poured
sugar on the fruit
and then mixed it with the cream.
"Do you want the spatula, my pet?"
said the woman.
"Yes, please!"
said the girl, and licked it clean.
Mmmmm.

They carried the blackberry fool to a wooden icebox stocked with blocks of ice they had delivered each day.

After Sunday dinner—potato soup, roast chicken and canned asparagus on toast—they spooned the fool into green dishes and ate it together with Father and the younger brothers. Even the baby had some.

Mmmmm. Mmmmm. Mmmmm.

Back in the kitchen, the girl ran her tongue along the inside of the bowl.

What a fine dessert!

Just a couple of years ago, in a city called San Diego, California, a boy and his dad bought two cardboard boxes of blackberries and a carton of pasteurized organic cream at the supermarket.

PUSH

When they got home, the man printed out a recipe from the Internet.

The boy beat the cream with an electric mixer.

Zzzzzzzzzh.

Two minutes later:
whipped cream.

It reminded the boy
of shaving foam.

The man ran water in the sink and
washed the berries in a colander.
He crushed them in a food processor,
then pushed them through a sieve
with a plastic spatula. Together, they
poured sugar on the fruit and then
mixed it with the cream.

"Can I lick the spatula?"
asked the boy.

"Course you can, buddy,"
said the man.

So the boy did.

Mmmmm.

They put the mixture in the refrigerator.

The doorbell rang and friends surged in, bringing cartons of lemonade, grilled vegetables, enchiladas and tomato salad.

After a long, good dinner, the man and his son spooned the blackberry fool into white dishes and served it to their guests.

Everyone gobbled it up. Especially the babies.

Mmmmm. Mmmmm. Mmmmm.

After the guests went home, the boy stood in the messy kitchen, licking the inside of the bowl.

What a fine dessert!

(But the blackberry fool had been so very, very delicious, there wasn't much left.)

A FINE DESSERT

Blackberry Fool: A Recipe

2-1/2 cups fresh blackberries (Other berries will do—but the fool won't be such a nice purple color; frozen berries will work, though fresh are nicer.)
1/2 cup sugar, divided in two
1 teaspoon vanilla
1-1/2 cups heavy cream

Find an adult to cook with you.

Mash the berries with a potato masher or a large fork. If you've got a food processor, you can use that. With clean hands, press the crushed berries through a sieve to remove the seeds. Sprinkle the fruit with 1/4 cup of the sugar. Stir.

In a separate bowl, mix together the remaining 1/4 cup of sugar, the vanilla and the cream. Using a whisk or whatever kind of beater you have, whip the mixture until it makes soft peaks, but not stiff ones.

Fold the sugared berries into the whipped cream. Taste it to see if it's sweet enough. Add more sugar if you need it. There should be streaks of white and purple.

Refrigerate for 3 hours or more.

Eat! And don't forget to lick the bowl.

A Note from the Author

A Fine Dessert raises some topics you may want to discuss, adults and children together. I hope the book inspires conversations.

This story includes characters who are slaves, even though there is by no means space to explore the topic of slavery fully. I wanted to represent American life in 1810 without ignoring that part of our history. I wrote about people finding joy in craftsmanship and dessert even within lives of great hardship and injustice—because finding that joy shows something powerful about the human spirit. Slavery is a difficult truth. At the end of the book, children can see a hopeful, inclusive community.

A less painful but still important topic is the history of women and girls in the kitchen and the feminization of domestic work: it would have been unlikely before the end of the twentieth century to see a father and son making dessert, as they do at the end of this story.

Children may easily recognize the changes in food preparation technology but with encouragement will also notice other changes that happened with time.

Fruit fool is one of the oldest desserts in Western culture. It dates back to the sixteenth century. The word *fool* most likely originated from the French word *fouler*, which means "to mash" or "to press"—so the name doesn't mean "silly fool"; it means "smushed-up." A fool can be made with any fruits but traditionally features tart ones: raspberries, gooseberries, blackberries, or rhubarb.

Details of the kitchen gadgets and the types of refrigeration are as accurate as I could make them. Two useful websites are The Food Timeline (foodtimeline.org) and Feeding America: The Historic American Cookbook Project (http://digital.lib.msu.edu/projects/cookbooks/). The rotary beater was patented in 1856. Before that, cream was whipped by hand. Electric mixers first appeared in homes around 1919 but did not become common until later. Food processors arrived in home kitchens in the 1970s. You'll notice that the cream is pasteurized only in the later kitchens, and that the twentieth-century family is the first to have an electric refrigerator. Pasteurization was invented in the 1860s, and the first home fridges appeared in 1911.

This book is about the connection of human beings to one another and to delicious flavors in the kitchen. No matter their circumstances, technologies, and methods of food sourcing, people have the same urge to lick the bowl!

Sources

Colquhoun, Kate. *Taste: The Story of Britain Through Its Cooking*. New York: Bloomsbury, 2007.

Hooker, Richard J. *Food and Drink in America: A History*. Indianapolis: Bobbs-Merill, 1981.

Mason, Laura. *Food and Culture in Great Britain*. Westport, CT: Greenwood Press, 2004.

Root, Waverly, and Richard de Rochemont. *Eating in America: A History*. New Jersey: Ecco, 1981.

Segan, Francine. Interview with the author, November 3, 2009.

Tannahill, Reay. *Food in History*. New York: Crown, 1988.

A Note from the Illustrator

It took me a year to make these drawings, though I wasn't drawing the whole time. Before I even sharpened my pencil, I made a twig whisk to see how it felt to whip cream in 1710. (My arm ached, and a few twiggy bits wound up in the cream, but it worked!) I made the dessert, and I ate it, of course. Then I began my research.

I visited the Victoria and Albert Museum in London to look at fabric patterns from the 1700s. I read slave owners' diaries from the 1800s. I thumbed through furniture catalogs from the 1900s, and I trawled San Diego real estate websites to find the perfect 2010 house.

I came up with a long list of questions: When are blackberries in season in Lyme, so I could dress my characters appropriately? (They are at their peak in late August.) Without photographs to guide me, how could I find out what slaves in 1810 Charleston wore on their feet? (From diaries, I learned that some went barefoot; others wore leather shoes handed down from their masters. I opted for shoes.) Since our 1910 family in Boston is sitting down to Sunday dinner, could they have bought their berries at a market earlier that day? (No, labor laws forbade businesses to open on Sundays. So I gave the mother and daughter one set of clothes for Saturday market and a second for Sunday best.)

Some questions were more difficult to answer: How did the slave girl feel, waiting on the family in 1810? And how did the other girl, roughly the same age, feel about being waited on?

After the questions came decisions. Around 1710 in England, there was, apparently, a brief fashion trend for wealthy men to dress like peasants, which I thought would be confusing. Our Lyme family is moderately wealthy, so I decided to give them moderately fancy clothes. On a plantation like the one in 1810, there probably would have been kitchen slaves to cook and house slaves to serve at table, but I thought it was more engaging—and not implausible—to follow one mother and daughter. And in real life, blackberry bushes are thick and tangled, but I was inspired by delicate 1800s botanical illustrations.

After I'd painted the last dot on the last page, I squished blackberries through a sieve with a spoon and used the purple juice to paint the endpapers. With the leftover blackberries, I made the fine dessert and I served it to my family. And the very last thing I did? I licked the bowl.

You can find out more about the process of illustrating *A Fine Dessert* at sophieblackall.com/illustration/books.